Can I Play Too?

Noelle Lambert

First published 2006 by
Veritas Publications
7/8 Lower Abbey Street
Dublin 1
Ireland
Email publications@veritas.ie
Website www.veritas.ie

ISBN 978 1 85390 944 3

A catalogue record for this book is available from the British Library.

Illustrated by Ronan Kennedy

Designed by Paula Ryan

Printed in the Republic of Ireland by Betaprint, Dublin

Veritas books are printed on paper made from the wood pulp of managed forests.
For every tree felled, at least one tree is planted, thereby renewing natural resources.

In loving memory of
my aunt, Breda Doyle,

an inspirational
person and teacher.

Down in the park

underneath the

tall trees

is a special

place,

a magical place,
where ...

all dogs play!

Every day dogs gather

to bark and to dig,

to sniff and to roll

and to play hide and seek.

Scamp is the champ

at catching his tail.

But Bruno leads the way

when they play race and chase.

One day a new dog came to town.

Sage Silka Sandy was his name –

Sandy for short!

A lively dog, a neat dog,

he barked a friendly question:

'Woof, woof, can I play too?'

All the dogs stopped.

'Yes,' they replied. 'Join in.'

'Come on. Let's run.'

But Bruno shook his head and said,

'I don't like him.'

'I don't like the shape of his face,' he said.

'He's different from us.'

'Huh?'

'What?'

 'Ugh?'

'What d'ya mean?'

'You cannot play with us,'

Bruno growled,

and Sandy crawled away.

The next day Bruno held a meeting.

'I don't like Snowy,' he said.

'She's too fluffy and she digs small holes.'

So Snowy crept away.

Bruno said,

'No more slow dogs,

no more short tails,

no more long ears,

no more spots.'

Bruno said,

'Only strong, fast dogs belong.'

And the park became
a tough place,

a scary place,

where no dog wanted to play.

Down on the beach

Snowy met Sandy

and Snowy saw that Sandy's eyes were friendly.

So Snowy said, 'Let's play!'

Snowy and Sandy howled a message

across the town

and the message said,

'Ruff, ruff. All dogs can play!'

Down on the beach
beside the big rocks,

is a marvellous place,
a happy place,
where all the dogs play.

Bruno came on down
and said, 'Can I play too?

I'm sorry. I was wrong.'
Sandy said, 'Yes.'

Snowy said, 'Yes. All dogs belong.'

They played together,

tried out their favourite games and ...

... they had a wonderful time!